Cover and internal design © 2015 by Sourcebooks, Inc.
Cover illustrations © Sesame Workshop
Text by Lillian Jaine
Illustrations by Joe Mathieu

Sourcebooks and the colophon are registered trademarks of Sourcebooks, Inc.

Published by Sourcebooks Jabberwocky, an imprint of Sourcebooks, Inc.
P.O. Box 4410, Naperville, Illinois 60567-4410
(630) 961-3900
Fax: (630) 961-2168
www.jabberwockykids.com

Library of Congress Cataloging-in-Publication
data is on file with the publisher.

Source of Production: Worzalla, Stevens Point, WI
Date of Production: March 2015
Run Number: 5003558

Printed and bound in
the United States of America.

WOZ 10 9 8 7 6 5 4 3 2

JUST ONE YOU!

by Lillian Jaine
illustrated by Joe Mathieu

123
SESAME STREET

sourcebooks
jabberwocky

This is a story that's all about you,
and all the **spectacular** things that you do.

So please come along and we'll show you it's true—
there is just one and only wonderful YOU!

Look all around, and here's what you'll find:
You are **unique!** You're one of a kind!

The **smile** on your face is like no smile I've seen.
You're one special person, if you know what I mean.

Your mind's full of **magic** to thrill and delight!
Even on dark days, you make the world bright!

No job is too **big**; no task is too **small**.
No matter what comes, you tackle it all!

You're strong and you're brave;
you're a grand **super hero**.
You give one hundred percent;
you never give zero!

You dance and you **dream**
from dusk until dawn.
Don't ever stop trying!
We'll cheer you on!

Your **adventures** may take you
away from your home,
but your best friends will be there
wherever you roam.

HOORAY FOR YOU!

Everyone knows how terrific you are.
We've always been sure that you will go **far!**

Because even if something doesn't quite go your way,

you will turn things **around** the very next day!

You're **perfect** as you—there's no one who's better!
So be true to yourself, and always remember. . .

There is just **one** you.
No other person does the things that you do.

Yes, it's absolutely, positively true.
There's just one and only wonderful **you!**